Dinno's Adventure And Other Tales

Mary-Ann Storm

Published by Mary-Ann Storm, 2023.

This is a work of fiction. Similarities to real people, places, or events are entirely coincidental.

DINNO'S ADVENTURE AND OTHER TALES

First edition. June 24, 2023.

Written by Mary-Ann Storm.

Table of Contents

Dinno's Adventure

Dinno laughs as he splashes water at his brother using his trunk. The herd were all basking in the sun while enjoying the water at the same time.

He couldn't hide his amusement once he noticed his brother was hiding behind their mother, who was openly annoyed at Dinno, who was very pleased with himself at his attempts.He was now looking around and realized the grown-ups were very caught up in their conversations.

This was one opportunity he wasn't going to miss. He knew he might never get an opportunity like this again. He made sure that no eyes were fixed on him as he slowly started to move away from the herd. Getting caught was not an option. He stole one last glance at the herd as he was about to enter the woods.

No one speaks about the woods. One thing they agree upon is the dangers that lurk in it, so everyone knows never to enter it. His little brother was shaking his head at him, letting him know that he mustn't enter the woods. His eyes were huge and Dinno knew it was because he was scared for his sake.

He hesitated . "Dinno, don't stray, stay close, it's dangerous to just wander off. Once you're bigger, you'll understand!"

These were the words his mother said to him regularly.

The only problem was he wanted to know what mysteries the woods held. There was no turning back now.

"Gmmmpf bigger! I am bigger," he shouted angrily at himself for doubting himself when he was supposed to be beside himself with happiness.

He anxiously looked around him, fearing that his mother might appear at any moment in his excitement. He forgot to be cautious. Once it dawned on him that he was still alone, he rushed on, not wanting to get caught, his adventure still awaited.

"Where are you going little one?"

Dinno almost shrieked out loud but soon realized the voice belonged to a bird who was sitting in a tree.

"I'm on my way to explore the woods" Dinno boasted proudly.

" Oh no little one go back to your herd!" chirped the bird as it flew away.

Dinno was very angry and disappointed this was not how his journey was supposed to start.

"Why should I? There's nothing dangerous about these woods!" he mumbled.

He stomped his feet in frustration and made a lot of noise in the process as he went along his way.

Dinno ran so fast that he failed to notice the Giraffe and bumped into it.

" Who dared to step on my foot!"

The Giraffe took his head down from the tree tops and noticed Dinno.

"Where's your herd, little one? Don't you know you're not supposed to wander off alone into these woods? The monster with the big teeth might catch you."

Dinno couldn't believe what he was hearing. "I've never heard of these monsters before."

As soon as he spoke the words he realized he was curious and wanted to know more.

"These monsters," continued the Giraffe, "has a silver sheen and very sharp teeth. They hide themselves under the grass and catch you once you step on them and from them, you rarely escape ."

"These monsters sound strange," Dinno replied cheekily.

"They may sound strange, still, it's best to avoid them and remember to never step on them." replied the Giraffe.

Dinno felt more confused than ever. "So they never move, they just remain in one place?"Dinno inquired, surprised.

"Why yes, that's why they are so smart."Answered the Giraffe patiently.

"Well, don't worry, I'm fast and I'll outrun them, " and off he went, not listening to the Giraffe anymore.

"Wait come back !" shouted the Giraffe.

He was really worried now, the little one didn't know the monsters were cleverly concealed underneath the grass most of the time.

Dinno couldn't believe his luck. He was warned to stay out of the woods because of monsters that couldn't even move. Dinno was so lost in thought he almost placed his foot on the Tortoise.

"Don't you dare put those huge feet of yours on me!"Shouted the Tortoise.

He quickly followed with another question.

"What are you doing here ?" Asked the Tortoise.

Dinno, on the other hand, was becoming impatient.

"Mr Tortoise, I would appreciate it if you could move faster."

"Faster! "The Tortoise asked disbelievingly.

"I'm going as fast as I can. What's your hurry anyway?" Dinno didn't want to explain that he wanted his exploring expedition to be over before his parents discovered that he was gone.

"It's very strange, you know," said the Tortoise.

"What is it ?" Dinno asked, showing his impatience.

"You walk around on your own, you're usually all together ."

Dinno couldn't believe it, not again what was so strange about him being out on his own?

"Well, I'm grown now," Dinno stated proudly.

"Oh, I don't know. You won't be grown enough for the noise monsters," answered the Tortoise knowingly.

"Noise monsters, I've never heard of them before," once again Dinno realized he wanted to know more.

"Oh it's terrible you never return when the noisy monsters get hold of you," answered the Tortoise.

Dinno couldn't believe what he was hearing. If you could hear the noise of the monsters then there, wouldn't be a problem, he thought.

"Don't worry, Mr Tortoise, my ears are big enough. Once I hear the noise of monsters, I'll just run away," and off he went.

"Wait!" The Tortoise shouted.

Dinno was too far away. The Tortoise knew he'd never be able to catch Dinno. To tell him that the noise monsters are silent at first, it's only afterward that you hear the noise.

Dinno was convinced that the woods were harmless. He couldn't understand what the fuss was all about. His attention was suddenly drawn to a deer running towards him in a panicked state. At the same time, he heard a very loud noise. It scared him so much that he stood transfixed in one spot.

"Run little one run, the noise monsters are coming !" The Deer shouted.

That got Dinnos' attention and he turned around and was running like the Deer. Behind them, the noise just intensified. It seemed so close to Dinno, that he finally understood why the woods were so dangerous.

"Dinno! " He heard his mother calling his name

She saw Dinno and gestured for him to come closer. The herd was already running towards the others warning them about the danger. It was complete chaos. The elders cleared the way for the ones that followed, trees fell in all directions as they ran towards safety.

Dinno couldn't tell how long it took before they were told to stop and rest. Everyone was relieved when they realized that they couldn't hear the noise of monsters anymore.

"Dinno, did you learn your lesson now ?" Asked his mother sternly.

Dinno felt bad just thinking about the noise. The monsters scared him all over again. Sighing, he flapped his big ears in designation accepting responsibility for his actions.

"Don't worry Mom, I'll never go near the woods again or go anywhere without you and Dad. Not until I'm really big enough, I promise."Came his curt reply.

They started their journey again to ensure that they'd be as far away from the monsters.

The Magical Nuts

Only Paws was visible underneath the green leaves, an occasional sound of protest was heard from the little figure focused on his task underneath the oak tree.

"Hey are you stuck, do you need help ?" A squeaky voice worriedly inquired.

Pats the Squirrel was torn between ignoring and acknowledging the other. With a sigh, he decided on the latter.

He carefully wriggled himself from the leaves while making sure his find was hidden from prying eyes. Once he turned, he was surprised to find an Ant whose worrisome frown was quickly replaced by a pair of curious eyes that rested on him very intently. The Ant kept on looking behind Pats as if he expected something to jump out.

"Thank you, as you can see, I'm quite fine," Pats replied hurriedly.

He quickly looked around to make sure there wasn't anyone near them who could overhear their conversation.

"I can see that now it looks more like you're hiding something." Answered the Ant.

" No! No! nothing, I'm just busy collecting my food for the winter."

Pats tried very hard not to look guilty as he told the lie.

"Well, then I'll be on my way." Said the Ant.

The Ant was already disappearing in the distance before Pats could reply. He had to admit he wasn't completely honest, the nuts did not belong to him.

Quite frankly, he'd never laid his eyes on anything like it. These were different types of nuts. They were gold and sparkled. All he knew was that he was keeping them. He had to get away before the owner arrived since he didn't know who the owner was. He rushed from the forest while he kept the nuts hidden from view.

Once he reached his house, he placed his find on the table, admiring it, and was glad no one was there to interrupt him. He lifted it to take a closer look. It was still sparkling. He couldn't wait to taste it, so he took a bite. It was the most delicious nut he'd ever tasted. It melted in his mouth.

His stomach was full, lazily he sat in his chair very happy at what he had found. He felt disappointed that he couldn't share his findings. Suddenly, he felt very tired and couldn't keep his eyes open, and fell asleep.

He barely slept and awoke with a jolt realizing the house seemed to be moving. Pats was now fully awake. He realized he was no longer in the safety of his house. The biggest dinosaur he'd ever seen almost flattened him against the ground.

They barely noticed him as they rushed over him. He ran as fast as he could to get out of the way. The Forest was in front of him and he ran towards it. It had the greenest trees and lakes, and the flowers and mountains were as beautiful. It was so quiet where he stood, he pinched himself just to make sure that he wasn't having a nightmare.

"Ouch! It's not supposed to hurt ." Pats mumbled to himself.

"I'm not sure what to make of you and to make matters worse, you're speaking to yourself."

The voice sounded very close. This time he didn't have time to scream. The creature spoke again, and the wind that came out of his mouth sent Pats flying through the air. Pats landed a few feet from the creature and saw that it was one of the Dinosaurs he'd seen earlier. The Dinosaur was now angry and annoyed and was venting his frustration for everybody to hear.

Pats knew he had to get away. As he ran he heard the Dinosaur and knew he was being followed. He was moving as fast as he could, realizing in panic he hadn't met anyone else besides the Dinosaur.

It took even longer before he realized the earth no longer shook beneath his paws. He was feeling drowsy and very tired and fell asleep as soon as he closed his eyes.

In his drowsy state, he was certain that he heard an Eagle and the sound was louder this time. He knew he had to get away but didn't want to make any sudden movements. When he finally got the courage to look up, He couldn't believe what he saw and that he had to run again.

It was the biggest Eagle he'd ever seen, and there was no mistaking the claws either. The bird's attention was on him. With its claws outstretched, it came flying down ready to grab Pats as soon as it was near enough. The other birds joined in chasing Pats.

He didn't wait any longer and ran as fast as his paws could carry him. All he wanted was to be hidden from view. The best choice he had was the big bush in front of him and it was within his reach.

He jumped in. In fear he saw how they circled above him, looking for any movement. Pats was sure they could hear how his heart was beating. He was relieved to see them giving up. Again he felt tired and decided it was time to rest as it was getting dark.

He had barely dozed off when an earth-shattering roar awoke him. Disappointedly, he realized somehow he was in another strange place. This time he was looking at the Tigers. They were also very big. The sight of them frightened Pats.

Some were in the trees, while some were lying on the grass in the sun. He couldn't help it, he shrieked and realized too late that the attention was now drawn towards him. One of the Tigers roared. Pats knew it was no friendly roar. The Tiger's teeth gleamed in the sunlight and Pats knew he wasn't waiting around to find out what the roar meant.

He was so tired of running he was missing his family and friends and just wanted to be home again. As he ran he knew his attempt was in vain. The Tiger was faster and just as its paw was about to grab Pats he felt himself becoming drowsy again and he panicked.

"I promise, I'll never do something like this again!" He yelled at no one in particular.

He no longer cared, it seemed the Tigers' paws were unavoidable and he closed his eyes.

Something kept on falling on his face and he realized he must've dozed off again. In the distance, he heard birds chirping. Pats was too scared to open his eyes. Again something landed on his face. He opened his eyes and saw that it was a leave. Pats sat up straight. He knew this area about that he was certain. He didn't want to be happy for no reason.

As soon as he recognized the tree, he knew he was home. The tree was the same one where he had found the nuts. He quickly searched for the leaves and there were the nuts. Pats were not even tempted to take them again. He was just relieved to be home. Quickly he covered them again and ran home to his family and friends.

Spot

Spot barks with excitement as he watches them driving off towards their holiday destination. He was chosen and everyone heard what the farmer said. Spot couldn't help it. He felt proud of himself.

He turned and looked at the farm yard. It was clear that he was regarded as the best and most important. Why else was he picked to be in charge of the rest?

Spot decided that he was going to make the farmer proud of him and make sure the farmer knew that he was the best guarding dog there ever was. He carried himself very proudly and confidently as he made his way to the front door of the house.

He surveyed the yard and decided that the inspection of the yard would start tomorrow. Spot made sure that he was the first one up the next morning. He made sure no unwelcome visitors had entered the yard or meddled with the fences. He didn't notice Stix the Chicken scuffling about doing his morning chores.

"Good morning Spot," greeted Stix cheerily.

Spot ignored Stix. He was important now. He couldn't believe that Stix had failed to remember that. He walked on, tail in the air, passing Stix. He was so annoyed at Stix so much so that he barked at the other puppies so that they could get out of his way.

Stix couldn't believe what he had seen. Something was wrong with Spot, or he was just having a bad day. He decided to warn the others of Spots' strange behavior.

The next morning it became clear to everyone that Spot had drastically changed overnight. He was issuing orders and telling them how they must be behaving. They decided to keep a close eye on Spot just in case it wasn't a passing phase.

Spot was very proud of himself, everyone was listening to him. Maybe not everyone, he thought to himself as he noticed pig prints on the front porch. He was very mad as he marched towards the pig camp below the house of the farmer.

"Oink! Oink!" He heard the funny bantering of the pigs with one another. They were rolling in the mud, enjoying themselves. They looked up and saw Spot looking at them.

One thing was clear to them. Spot was not in a very pleasant mood. Spot was very angry with them, he didn't even know how stern he looked from their view.

"Starting from today, until the farmer comes back, there'll be no straying towards the house" Spot informed them in barks.

The pigs weren't as understanding as Stix the Chicken.

"What happens if we don't listen to you!" They Oink dismissively at him.

Spot couldn't believe what he was hearing.

"Since I'm in charge, I'll just have to tell the farmer about your behavior and he'll have to decide your fate!"

Although the pigs wanted to argue further, they decided against it. Who knew what the farmer might do?

Disobeying Spot, it seems, would get them into serious trouble. They all decided that whatever plagued Spot was going to be a problem until the farmer returned.

Together they decided Spot was no longer fun to be around. They decided that they'd just ignore Spot. Eventually, Spot gave up any attempts at issuing orders or trying to make conversation. Spot knew what they were trying to do. He was fine with it, he was important now.

As hard as he tried, he couldn't stick to his decision.

After considering it for a long time, he decided that having fun, conversations, and playing with friends was what made him happy. He didn't want to be important anymore, he just wanted to be one of the guys and did just that.

Sorbra And Tin's Sea Adventure

The waterfall poured down in blue rays, landing in the stream below. Just above it sat the two friends, Sorbra the Lion and Tin the Leopard. Sorbra was eyeing Tin with a challenging glance, knowing he couldn't waver at all. Tin would see it as a sign of weakness.

He couldn't believe that he had allowed himself to be goaded into a dare by Tin, though he had to admit he hadn't been challenged like this for a long time and he couldn't deny that it felt great. He didn't like the idea of the waterfall underneath the tree trunk.

Sorbra knew the challenge would be less daring if not for the waterfall. Sorbra didn't see how he could fail at a challenge that he could master with his eyes closed. Crossing to the other side of the waterfall wouldn't be a problem.

" I'll do this on one condition. That is if you join me." Sorbra threw Tin's challenge back at him.

Sorbra could see Tin didn't like the idea of him being outmaneuvered like that.

"We don't have to do it if you're scared ." Sorbra continued mockingly.

He pointed towards the treetrunk with a smile. While he eyed the waterfall, he smiled with a knowing glance at Tin.

"No way! , besides I'm a natural at this. I just want to spare you any humiliation."Tin replied with confidence.

Sorbra never backed out of a challenge and he wasn't about to start now. He made sure Tins were following him as he started towards the tree trunk.

Sorbra walked with pride and knew he wasn't about to miss a challenge that was thrown at him. It didn't stop his eyes from wandering to the waterfall below them.

The tree trunk was moving uncontrollably and he realized it was due to Tin, who couldn't keep still. It wasn't long before he heard Tins' screams and Sorbra looked back to see what was going on. Bees were obscuring Tins' view, who was trying to chase them away though he wasn't succeeding at all.

It wasn't long before he had the same problem. As hard as he tried, he couldn't chase them away and he lost his footing in the process.

Tin saw what was happening and tried to stall Sorbra's fall. Without success, they were both plunging towards the waterfall screaming but knowing they were helpless to do anything.

Only roaring sounds were heard as they landed on the waterfall right on a strong current. There was nothing they could hold on to, while the current only became stronger.

"What now?" Tin shouted above the waves.

Sorbra didn't have time to answer. His eyes were fixed on a spiraling vortex in a ray of color that was headed their way. He knew once it reached them they'd be sucked in.

Tin was no longer trying to get his attention and he knew Tin was worried about the vortex too. He turned to make sure he was right and heard Tins' warning.

"Watch out!" Tin shouted at him.

It was too late. The waves carried them further into the vortex.

"Sorbra! Sorbra !" Tin was anxiously calling his name.

He opened his eyes and saw Tin, who was trying to wake him. Sorbra could only stare in awe and confusion at what he saw. They were underneath the water somehow breathing as if they were walking on land.

The water was different too. It had the bluest crystalline sheen Sorbra had ever seen. Plants in a ray of colors were held in place by the rocks.

Seashells and oysters were laid around while the fishes swam. Only a few of the fishes looked at them and appeared to be anxious.

They scurried away with no warning as to why they were fleeing. Sorbra and Tin heard their hushed conversation as they swam away.

"What an odd way to greet someone," Tin murmured in awe.

" I'd like to know where we are and how we ended up here," Sorbra replied.

" I have no idea, but I'm sure we'll find out soon enough," Tin answered.

Sorbra knew Tin was referring to the fish, a dark shade covered the water and Sorbra knew they'd have their answer soon enough because even the temperature of the water had changed.

When Sorbra and Tin looked up at the stirring sounds caused by the water, a big shark came into view, it swam towards them. Its teeth bared, and an ugly scar covered its face. Its whole posture appeared threatening, as were the ones which followed him.

They surrounded Sorbra and Tin with no room for escaping.

"Well! Well, what have we here? You guys are a long way from home." The Shark bit out.

Sorbra didn't like his tone or attitude and knew whomever this Shark was, he was bad news. He signaled Tin not to lose his temper.

"If you could show us the quickest way out of here, we'd be out of your way ." Tin challenged the Shark.

Sorbra knew Tin couldn't stand to be insulted in any way.

"It speaks!"

The Shark taunted them further while bowing insultingly in front of them. It caused the other Sharks to come closer in a threatening stance.

Sorbra knew things were becoming worse for them. Especially when he saw out of the corner of his eye two fishes hiding behind a cactus, viewing the scene before them with sympathy.

" What are you waiting for, Scar!"

One of the Sharks impatiently urged their leader into action. Scar didn't like to be rushed or interrupted, it seemed, as he turned in anger to the one who spoke. It immediately caused the Shark to hang its head in obedience, the rest took a few paces backward.

Sorbra knew that meant Scar was the leader of them.

"Grab them!" Scar gave them the order.

They had no choice but to obey. In numbers, they wouldn't stand a chance.

" I guess it's too late to tell you, I'm sorry about the stupid dare," Tin mumbled only for Sorbra to hear.

"No need for apologies. I accepted the challenge, didn't I? Let's just make it out of this in one piece." Sorbra answered.

It was obvious that they shouldn't expect any help from anyone. They were led to a dark rock-centered entrance.

"Get in!" Scar ordered them.

Again they just obeyed. As the rock entrance closed behind them. They knew they weren't going anywhere, but still, they had to find a way out.

They had noticed the curious eyes as they were led to the room. All they knew was they couldn't remain there.

"I can't believe that we're in this mess."Tin finally voiced his disappointment.

Sorbra knew the feeling, but giving up was the last thing they should do.

"Don't you give up, there's a way out. We just haven't found it yet."Sorbra encouraged him.

As he spoke, he went to every part of the room looking for an escape route. Outside, the cheering and celebrating went on.

"They are celebrating their catch, it seems," Tin spoke with sarcasm.

"That, my friend, is exactly what we need," Sorbra answered him.

Sorbra noticed that light was filtering through, the surface was sand. He showed Tin, who started to dig beside him. Once the hole was big enough, they placed a flat stone on top, while Sorbra climbed through, which was quickly followed by Tin.

He got out just in time before the sand sank back, closing the hole. It was dark outside and they were guided by the plants that shone like lanterns in the night sky.

"It seems they haven't discovered that we're gone," Tin said happily.

"That's great for us. The longer they party, the more time we get to seek help and get out of here." Sorbra replied.

They kept on walking when Tin decided to take a closer look at a plant making musical sounds. He was so close to the plant it almost sucked him in. Sorbra had to pull on him so he could be free. The music from the plant grew louder and louder.

It finally stopped once a shamefaced Tin landed beside Sorbra in tiredness. They decided to stay clear of everything to stay safe. That's when they noticed the cheering and celebrating couldn't be heard anymore. They moved faster because they knew time was against them.

"We're free. There's the woods!"Tin yelled with relief.

Sorbra hesitated for the woods to appear just like that out of nowhere had him worried.

"Isn't it better to check first?"Sorbra asked.

"There's no need there it is.Let's just enter it so we can go home, " Tin replied hurriedly.

They saw how the sky lit up behind them and the sudden movement of the water. Sorbra needed no encouragement, he knew who was on the way towards them. As soon as they entered the wood, the image disappeared.

They realized they were caught in a jelly balloon completely sealed off with them inside of it. Then it moved them up into the air. The sharks tried to break it without success and were left stranded in anger until they disappeared from their view. "Sorbra! "Tin yelled in alarm.

Sorbra didn't answer him, he knew they had to make sure, but no Tin had to get away and he was running from the Sharks. The balloon finally stopped and burst open, causing them to land hard on the surface.

They were inside a lighted room, filled with all kinds of fish in shapes and colors. They looked at them in a very unwelcoming manner. They swam closer and started to pull on them, they both roared in frustration at them, revealing their teeth.

They heard hushed conversations behind them. Sorbra recognized the little fish who was hiding from the Sharks. They were with the leader of the fish colony. They kept on speaking and looking in their direction. Everyone else fell silent as the leader approached them.

"What now?" Tin groaned.

Sorbra didn't have the energy to reply as he watched them approach.

"Take them to the leech dorm!"Ordered the giant fish.

Sorbra and Tin were once again outnumbered. They walked without resisting. As soon as they entered the room, the door closed behind them.

"This can't be happening, Sorbra. Thinking of something. " Tin whispered.

Sorbra didn't know what to do. All he knew was that the leeches must not be allowed near them. He was still wondering what to do, when the walls chimed out a melody in a rapid succession, then the door swung open.

"Follow me and be quick about it," came the curt order from the fish.

Sorbra and Tin needed no invitation. They moved as fast as they could, closing the door behind them, a lighted fish led the way for them and they followed in silence. They were led back to the meeting room. Inside. The dolphins are now the center of attention. Everyone cleared the way.

"Like I just said they came through the vortex by accident," Continued the Dolphin.

Sorbra couldn't speak or even ask how the Dolphin knew that.

"Do you know how we can go home?"Tin asked him.

"Sure I do, but we must move quickly. Just follow us." replied the friendly Dolphin.

They passed the lake of seashells and octopus space, crabs moved around while the fishes made way for them to pass through. Sea horses and starfishes happily waved at them.

They didn't go far when the two dolphins asked them to stop. Spinning with their tails, they blew into the white glowing seashells.

In front of their eyes, a vortex opened. The Dolphins gently pushed them into the vortex while they kept on blowing the seashells. This time they were awake and looked at the sphere of colours which surrounded them.

It was such a beautiful sight. They forgot why they were there. The colors disappeared and they realized they were back in the woods. They both looked at the tree trunk.

"No way! I'm not going through that again. " Said Tin. Sorbra just laughed. They both learned their lesson and just wanted to go home.

The Rabbit Who Didn't Fit In

Toby landed flat on his face. The mud changed his white fur to a brownish color. In haste, he decides to rub it, just wanting to be rid of it. After a while, he had to admit that it was a hopeless attempt.

The mud only spread further and he was making things worse than they already were. It didn't help matters. When he realized someone was finding his situation hilarious, it angered him and he decided to ignore whomever it was.

"Hey, dummy!" Yelled a very persistent little voice at him.

Toby almost groaned out loud in agony. Trixie, the mouse, is the biggest gossiper in the forest and the last person he wants around.

"Can't you see I'm busy ?" Toby mumbled.

He wished for once Trixie would know when to back off. Instead, he was greeted with another round of laughter and turned to confront Trixie. Who was rolling on the grass holding her stomach in a fit of giggles.

"Just wait! Wait till I tell the others." She yelled out.

"Toby the clutch did it again!" The taunting voice continued.

Toby knew that there was nothing he could do.

"Maybe it's because you've got one green eye and one brown eye, it must be out of focus," Trixie continued.

As always, it hurt to hear the words, though Trixie was oblivious to the impact it had on Toby. It was the same with the rest of his peers. Without realizing it, Toby angled his body into a proud stance, and with a rigid back, he started to move away from Trixie. The branches suddenly rustled and Toby immediately knew the reason behind its sudden movement. It was the famous trio: Pete the Bird, Bud the Crab, and Sam the Snake.

"Wow look at you!" Pete chirped.

He was already looking around himself to make sure that he had an audience. Toby knew that Pete was going to be his arrogant self and that he'd never hear the end of it. You wouldn't think that they all live in secluded Mirva, there's just no fellowship amongst them.

He didn't allow Pete to finish what he started, he hopped away instead.

He felt happy and relieved he was leaving the Forest and its problems behind him. The shouting and taunting subsided to nothing.

He was finally being honest with himself, it didn't matter how many times he braced himself not to feel offended by the jokes.

It seems his reaction to it wasn't getting better. In fact, given his response earlier, his reaction was worse than he'd thought it would be.

Toby was still running but slowed his pace once he saw the stream in front of him. He dived right in just wanting to get rid of the mud.

He suddenly wished he could wash his differentness away too. He had already noticed the Frog who'd been sitting on a leaf looking at him in curiosity.

He had chosen to ignore the Frog. He didn't want to make conversation with anyone. Once he was done, he jumped out again.

That's when he noticed the rippling effect of the water. He leaned closer to get a better look. What caught his attention was the reflection of himself in the water.

He noticed he hadn't quite hidden his unhappiness. His shoulders and ears were hanging in a hopeless gesture and his eyes showed his unhappiness quite prominently.

He was tired of being different, everywhere he looked they were all the same except him. His tears were dripping into the pond, he didn't care who saw him at that moment, he was openly crying now.

What made matters worse was, that his parents brothers, and sisters were also cautious around him. The Frog was now staring at him. He didn't avoid eye contact either. He knew the questions about his eyes would follow.

Before the Frog could start with the questions he hopped away. Toby realized he was more furious with himself than anyone else and he decided he didn't need anyone. He can make it on his own.

He was out of breath and very tired when he finally stopped. He took shelter in the shade of a rock and for the first time, he noticed his surroundings.

The area was unknown to him and it appeared haunted and very dark. He wanted to forget everything and just go home. He rejected the thought as soon as it came to mind.

For him, nothing could be worse than what he left behind. Toby was not at ease, it was getting darker and he still hadn't found a place to sleep.

That's when he noticed a small hole at a distance, hopping closer he peered in. The hole was empty and Toby couldn't pick up any danger from the inside so he went in.

He was glad that he could find a place inside the tree trunk that concealed the entrance and it made him even happier and he felt free. He didn't feel like an outcast anymore, he made it so far and things could only get better.

The beautiful sound of birds singing awoke him the next morning. Outside, his surroundings turned out to be more than what he'd thought. He was surrounded by green trees, and butterflies in all colors were flying around.

They were moving from one flower to the other. He stood in wonder and knew he was going to have the time of his life. Then it dawned on him he wasn't alone, a very angry and persistent little voice was vying for his attention.

"Hey, you! Move your big feet! Why do they have to be all over the place?"

Toby didn't reply, at first, too shocked and, secondly, he hadn't quite found the owner of the voice until he finally did so. To his amazement, he found a very angry worm on the ground and he was blocking its way.

"Get out of my way, I need to get to the sand near that stream!" The worm shouted at Toby.

Toby was very stunned and just moved out of the way. He was too curious to know what the reason was behind the worm's grumpiness.

"Mr Worm, why are you so angry?" asked Toby.

" I can't have a conversation with you right now, it'll be the end of me if I don't reach the stream in time, so get out of my way", came the sharp reply.

"Well, let me help you ." Offered Toby in remorse.

"No thank you, I don't need your pity, I'll find my way." Came the bitter reply.

Toby measured the distance to the stream from where he stood. He wasn't so sure the worm was going to make it. Toby moved out of the way. He didn't want to upset the worm any further. The worm carried so much anger in him.

.

For the first time, he was glad to have his mismatched eyes that didn't give him any problems like that.

He felt so happy and decided that he was going to explore his surroundings and down the road he went. He passed a field of flowers. It was the rainbow on display for Toby. He felt like dancing on his paws.

"Yep! Yeeppee !" Yelled Toby, just wanting to release some of his excitement.

He was having the time of his life, glad that for once he didn't have to be cautious. As he turned again, he wanted to make sure that what he saw wasn't a mistake on his part.

The black and white outlines of a skunk, Toby froze. There's a valid reason for avoiding skunks. The odor of a skunk has a way of staying on you for a long time and it's a stench no one can stand.

Toby was getting ready to run. The skunk approached Toby and he panicked. He instinctively moved backward. He kept his eyes on the skunk.

That's when he noticed that the skunk had a wary look in its eyes. Toby didn't want to know the reason behind the skunk's eyes. What he wanted was distance.

"Please Mr Rabbit, I only want to ask for directions."Pleaded the skunk.

Toby stopped. He wasn't sure if he could trust the skunk and remembered the times he felt so bad like the skunk and he remained where he was.

" I only want to know how long it is towards the stream. I'm thirsty. I know you want to get away from me and you have no idea how that feels."

Toby felt ashamed and guilty for behaving that way. He didn't want the skunk to know that.

"That's because of the way you smell. You would run too if you were me." Toby replied dryly.

The skunk looked disappointed in Toby and he sighed.

"That's only when they come too close and I have to protect myself."

Toby felt bad and he didn't want the skunk to pick up on it, so he pointed in the direction of the stream. Toby saw how the wariness was replaced by happiness as the skunk ran towards the stream.

Toby couldn't believe how he treated the skunk. He was not very proud of his actions towards the skunk.

So far, he had only met Mr Worm, who was too angry to ask for help. He was different because he moved so slowly, but his pride could cost him dearly.

The skunk reminded Toby of himself, but the skunk took the chance of being rejected when he asked for advice and he was the one who was happy in the end.

Toby finally admitted to himself that being different doesn't mean you're an outcast. It's how you perceive people's reactions towards you. What you see isn't the way other people see you.

His family loves him, but they may not always understand him and know what to do when it comes to him. He didn't want to end up like a worm but more like a skunk. It was time to go home.

He hopped towards his village and realized that no one was working. Instead, they were all surrounding his family, who looked very unhappy and worried.

At that moment, his mother looked up and saw him. The relief and happiness he saw on her face as well as the others' faces made him realize his differentness didn't matter, he was one of them, he just failed to see it.

The Unicorn That Stole The Rainbow

The chirping of the birds woke Ranger where he lay underneath the flowers. He was so angry at himself as he saw the butterflies and fairies flying around whilst the dwarfs were each attending to their chores that were set out for the day.

He couldn't believe that he overslept he wanted to show off the beautiful colorful stripes that adorned his nose. He wanted everyone's attention on him, he loved it when they were all looking at him admiring him, wishing they could all be like him as they always do. He was certainly the prettiest of the lot, he thought as he caught a glimpse of himself in the morning dew drop hanging from a leaf.

"Good morning you beautiful thing, are you ready to show them, just how much they must envy you?" Ranger boasted to himself.

"Aargh! Seriously Ranger it's way too early to be so self-absorbed!"Scolded poaksy the dwarf.

Ranger gave the dwarf an angry look as he aimed his nose in his direction as the magical heat stream moved from the tip of it. The dwarf shrieked in fear as he jumped out of the way landing in a puddle, fear was very evident in each move that he made. Ranger laughed throwing his head backwards.

The dwarf was such a comical sight, how dare he address a royal like him like that. He pointed at the dwarf again wanting to teach him a lesson, but a glimpse of the sunlight out of the corner of his eye made him realize that he'd be late for unicorn training, and that couldn't happen.

All of them must see how powerful he is now, he stomped his foot in the water and watched as it sprayed over the fear-stricken dwarf who was trying to get away from him.

"You little mud! Be glad that I have to be somewhere " He glaringly informed the dwarf.

The dwarf couldn't move and lifted his hand trying to ward off any hit that might come from the Unicorn. He couldn't see where the unicorn stood because his hands were in front of his eyes.

He finally decided to look when he realized nothing was happening, he peeped through his fingers and realized that it wasn't his imagination. His assumptions were correct about the unicorn. It did leave while he wasn't looking.

The dwarf dashed as he suddenly saw the shadow of a unicorn.

"No! No! Don't hurt me. I promise to keep my opinions to myself "The Dwarf called out in panic.

"Easy, Easy calm down nothing is going to happen to you". A calm voice instructed him

The dwarf looked up and realized that it was the King of the Unicorns who was observing him with worry and sympathy.

"Your majesty! My apologies I didn't see you" Stuttered the dwarf

"That's all right dwarf you had your hands full, all because of my son "Sighed The King.

His eyes looked in the direction where his son disappeared. A frown pleaded between his eyes as he turned back to the dwarf. He couldn't miss the other dwarves ' stricken faces.

They peeked from behind leaves in his direction. How did he miss what his son was busy with? He wondered if he was at fault for his son behaving like this.

"I'm fine your Majesty, thank you, the dwarf stuttered.

"I'm glad to hear that, "the King replied

He stepped forward lifted the dwarf from the puddle and gently put him on the grass. He then turned and flew into the air leaving behind a bright light the only proof that a unicorn was there.

Ranger landed on the training sight between the mountains, though to his surprise no one was there. The flowers and trees stood as beautiful as ever and the grass showed no sign of being walked on. Ranger became worried did the teacher say something and did he miss it he wondered.

"Where's everyone? " He asked in bewilderment.

"They all left for the kingdom of Splendour " chirped a bird sitting on a rock while its eyes curiously rested on Ranger.

"Splendour! You say" He enquired irritably.

He angrily lashed out at a tree splitting it in half with his unicorn light strike.

The bird flew away anxiously he knew being around an angry Unicorn was not a smart move. He watched as trees fell and the earth was struck open and shook his head at the scene beneath him glad that he flew just in time, not doubting that he would've been in the crossfire had he stayed.

Ranger was tiredly panting out of anger as he looked with slitted eyes in the direction of Splendour.

How dare they go without informing him. Ranger knew they went there to watch the vibrant colors of the rainbow. As they flew underneath its showers.

He'll show them nobody is going to steal his moment to shine. Ranger knew that the stripes on his nose were no match for the display of the rainbow. So he'll go there and take the rainbow away from them.

All he has to do is to find the light-bearers there are three of them. Then there'll be no rainbow for them and all the attention will be back where it should be on him. With a determined look on his face, Ranger flew towards the Kingdom of Splendour.

It was laughter and light that greeted Ranger as he landed in the Oasis of Merky. He became even angrier as he realized no one had noticed his arrival. How rude he decided, they even forgot that he must be shown respect at all times.

All this because of a Rainbow. He grimaced as he watched how the unicorns were so happy, he was enjoying the fact that their happiness and this beautiful place, would be gone in minutes and their happiness short-lived.

He quickly went to stand beneath the tree as he watched them. Ranger closed his eyes and activated his location power. Each of the light keepers was visible to him and he quickly threw a jolt in each direction and watched as each lightkeeper fell to the ground still keeping them in the grip of the lightning jolt he quickly moved them to the entrance of a wet darkened cave.

They were all unconscious. He knew he had to reach them before they awoke. As he flew off he didn't notice the darkness creeping in or the flowers that started to die, the ground that suddenly became dry as if it had suffered a drought for many years.

Nor did he pay attention to the shock and panicked outbursts of the Unicorns. Who was now fearing the worst wondering what terrible thing had befallen them.

Ranger landed in front of the cave and wondered about the sudden change in the trees and flowers but as soon as the thought came to mind he dismissed it.

He carried each light keeper into the cave and tied them up with a magical rope that could only be untied by a royal unicorn. He wanted to ensure that no one could interfere, or become a problem for him.

He walked out of the cave with a smile as he recalled the three light keepers not being able to free themselves, that'll certainly teach them to steal his chance to shine. His pretty sure no one would dare to challenge him. Besides they all knew who his father was.

As Ranger flew back he realized that there was a sudden change and he wondered what could be the reason behind it the light seemed to have vanished.

Everything had a look of doom around it every flower in the trees appeared to be dead. Even he felt cold and empty for no reason as if there were no warmth at all. What astonished him the most was that as he flew the same doom and gloom had spread to their kingdom too.

"Where have you been? Shouted Crimlog

Ranger didn't have the energy for his friend he wanted to know what happened, he feared that it might be something terrible. If it wasn't dangerous it wouldn't have affected them all in such a manner.

What worried him the most was that even his unicorn powers had suddenly vanished he was just like everyone else how could this be?

He gallops towards his father not paying attention to his friend anymore. All the unicorns gathered around his father. All the fairies dwarfs and even the Lion King were there.

"Quiet! Roared the Lion King

It was clear that something terrible had happened and they must be looking for the culprit.

All fell silent at his order. However, the worry and fear of their survival were etched onto all of them. It was clear that this was one enemy they did not know how to defeat. It caused them to fight with each other.

Yet they waited obediently to hear what the Lion King wanted to say.

"It came to my attention that one of you disturbed the order of balance by holding the light keepers captive ." shouted the Lion King

Ranger froze at the words as the crowd started to look at each other with anger and accusation ready to find out who it was.

"Wait! Before you start accusing each other". Came the curt order from The Lion King.

"The one responsible is a unicorn using his lightning power" Continued the Lion King

As soon as the words were said Ranger could feel his father's eyes on him as well as the anger which eroded from him.

"Ranger! Come here", his father shouted at him

Lightning struck as his father's anger intensified, the other animals scurried away in fear, looking for a hiding place. Everyone knew that you mustn't be near Unicorns when they're fighting. Only the Lion King remained in place, not wanting to miss anything.

"What did you do" Continued his father

"I'm sorry Father!" replied Ranger

"Just tell me what you did?" His father asked.

He was no longer angry at his son it was more disappointment than anything else.

"I hid them in a cave " Ranger replied

He was afraid of what his actions cost them, he didn't know everybody would be affected he just wanted the Kingdom of Splendour to suffer. Even worse he can't even use his horn with his new powers to show off. He didn't want to show off anymore he was more worried about the damage he had caused.

"Come and show me " his father ordered

They galloped towards the Kingdom of Splendour to free the light keepers. It took them longer to reach the cave. When they galloped into the cave the light keepers were awake and were worryingly looking at them. It appears they already knew the outcome of his selfishness.

"How are we supposed to free them?" Asked Ranger.

His father's sympathy towards his son grew. He knew that in his haste to boast about his newfound powers. He lost it the moment he got it and he didn't even know that the restraints could be broken with that very same horn without its powers.

"Don't worry son you can still break it by sowing it with your stripes, although it's very tiresome" His Father replied.

Ranger's father watched as he broke each magical rope until he tiredly fell to the ground. He felt sorry for his son but he knew he had to be taught that all actions have consequences and this was a very light punishment for what he had done to them all.

The lightkeepers looked at Ranger's father with respect and relief as they held each other's hands whilst vanishing in front of their eyes.

They walked out of the cave everything was still the same as they left it. Though as they galloped the sunshine broke through the darkness. The trees began to get their color back as well and the grass's beautiful flowers all came alive as every animal lifted their heads to feel the sun's rays on them filling them with happiness.

The dwarfs danced with each other as tears of happiness streamed down their faces. Ranger took it all in and he attempted to fly and realized that as he was reaching for the sky his powers were back again. He turned to look at his father who was looking at him with a smile. Ranger felt very ashamed at what he had done only because he wanted to be envied by everyone.

"I'm sorry Dad" Said Ranger.

Ranger's father knew that his son learned his lesson, a lesson that he would never forget. It was also a lesson that will shape him into a better ruler. A ruler with Empathy and fairness.

"I know son" replied his father.

They flew together towards their Kingdom. All the animals have dispersed, a sign that they were happy with the outcome of the journey of father and son.

"Father there's still something that I need to tend to" Ranger informed his father.

"You may go, just make sure you're home before nightfall" his father replied

Ranger flew and frantically looked for the dwarf he was so mean to. He watched as the dwarf wanted to make a run for it.

"No! Please wait" Ranger Shouted

That stopped the dwarf in his tracks an apologetic Ranger wasn't what he expected. The dwarf waited as Ranger landed in front of him.

"I'm sorry for being so mean," said Ranger

"That's okay your highness we all have our off days" The dwarf replied

The dwarf didn't know why the prince suddenly had a change of heart but he was thankful for it. He watched as he flew off. The other dwarfs came out of hiding. They couldn't believe what they'd just witnessed, although all of them were glad that they no longer had to fear the prince's presence anymore.

The Sparrow Who Made It Home

Scoops the Sparrow ruffled his feathers, in excitement while jumping up and down. Outside the cold winter breeze blew and everyone stayed close to each other. It was time for their journey south.

Scoops looked up to his mother and father and felt very proud. He was finally going to be part of the longest journey, everyone kept talking about.

Flying south is one of the most courageous things a young sparrow can do. There is a big celebration for all the new sparrows who made it south and medals are rewarded for the ones that do.

Scoops have heard many stories of sparrows who never made it home. That made him feel sad and worried. Although that didn't last long scoops' parents made sure of that.

As soon as he was strong enough to fly his parents made sure to take him along on their longest flying routes. They wanted to be sure that he would be ready for his journey south. His mother always told him at bedtime of their journeys south. At the ending of the story she'd look at him and say, that he had nothing to worry about he'd know how to reach the south if he'd ever get lost.

So Scoops was very excited. The journey certainly sounded amazing and he and his friends will also share in it. He looked in his friend's direction and saw that all of them were as excited as he was. That's when Grim their leader flew onto the tree trunk to address them all.

"Guys the time has finally come for our historic Journey to the south," said Grim in a proud manner.

An outburst of happy chirping greeted his words. It was clear that everyone was just as happy as they were. They hopped up and down showing just how they felt.

"Yes and it's my son's first time on this journey", shouted his father proudly.

"Ours too! " shouted the rest of them

The leader smiled and cautioned all with his wing to listen once more to what he had to say.

"As all you parents know, you must keep your little ones close and away from any dangers along the way." Their leader continued.

"Don't worry Grim! We'll protect our little ones they are too precious to us". One of the men assured him.

"And how do we fly? "Their leader shouted

"In one row " The crowd shouted back.

Their leader then turned and started to fly all that needed to be said was said. Scoops looked back and smiled it was a straight line. He looked down and couldn't believe how small everything looked from above. The trees looked so small but he loved the wind sweeping through his feathers and the blue sky above him.

They passed houses and fields roads and valleys sometimes mountains. What was most beautiful for Scoops was the other animals running below them.

Scoops didn't know how long they'd flown before dark clouds suddenly appeared strikes of lightning blurred his vision all of a sudden everything was covered in grey around Scoops as the rain lashed down on him. He couldn't see where his parents and the rest were.

Scoops frantically flapped his wings, hoping to clear his path, and bumped into something hard. It was an Eagle who looked down in anger at Scoops but still flew on without looking back. A sudden surge of panic gripped Scoops, what if he was all alone?

"Hello, guys! You can come out now " he shouted.

There was no one shouting back at him Scoops realized, that he might be right in fearing for the worst. He was so lost in thought that he didn't notice the sky was clear again.

As Scoops looked around him. It dawned on him that he was all alone and there was no one to help him to reach the south. He looked down to the trees and animals beneath him and wondered if he must go down and rest.

But then he thought if he went down how would he know in what direction to fly? Then his mother's words came to him.

" if you ever get lost at some point in time, whilst flying south just remember to follow your inner voice " his mother had said in her story.

Scoops looked and saw that the sun was in front of him and he made a u-turn out of joy he nearly bumped into a flock of doves passing by.

"Ooh you poor thing" how will you reach the south now" they asked him

But Scoops was not even saddened by their question. He knew now that all he had to do was to recall his mother's story.

" Oh don't worry about me! I'll be there in no time"He shouted back at them.

The Doves didn't believe a word. They feared the worst for this little Sparrow. The way they looked at him said it all. But Scoops was now full of confidence and kept his eyes on the sun. It wasn't long before he met a Blue crane.

"Wow, aren't you lost " The Blue crane grimaced at Scoops.

"No, I'm not! I know exactly where I'm going " replied Scoops

"I'm not so sure you'll ever make it how about joining me on my trip," Asked the Blue crane.

Scoops looked at the Blue crane and weighed his options. It would be nice to have someone to fly with and he would be sure that he'll reach his destination.

But then he thought of his mother and father and knew his mother told him the story in case he needed it someday. He wouldn't trade his parents for anything he'll just keep on thinking about his mother's story.

"No thank you, I know where I'm going " replied Scoops

"Okay if you say so, all the best to you," said the Blue crane

Scoops watched as the Blue crane flew away not worried that whatever he decided could've been wrong.

Suddenly Scoops heard a loud sound. It was so loud it scared him. He looked around him and saw nothing. He was very worried was there something that his mother could've left out he wondered.

He realized that a loud sound came from above him, and flew to the side. That's when he noticed it was a plane flying above him.

He sighed out of relief. His mother did mention planes and their harmless you just have to stay out of their way and not be squashed by them.

Again Scoops felt at peace and smiled and started his journey. Scoops didn't know how but he knew how to get to the south. He also realized that it would be night soon and he kept on flying till it became dark and made sure he found a safe spot. Away from any danger, his mother warned him against that too.

She also said if he must fly at night he must follow the stars, but Scoops was too tired he just wanted to rest for a while. Scoops awoke the next morning from a hissing sound and realized that it was a snake.

He got such a fright and just flew into the air. He wanted to find something to eat before he flew further. But he was too scared of the snake.

Scoops looked down and realized that below him was a very disappointed snake that followed his every move. Now that was one friend he didn't need Scoops thought as he flew in the opposite direction of the sun.

He crossed lots of mountains and valleys. Scoops decided to find some food as he was really hungry and saw a man in a park throwing seeds.

Scoops flew down and ate as much as he could that's when he saw the shadow of a cat its paw stretched out towards him and Scoops quickly flew out of its reach and into the sky.

The man and cat became little specs underneath him as Scoops flew as high as he could ready to start his journey again. Scoops was now very aware of the dangers of his journey as he flew underneath a blue sky.

That night Scoops decided it was best to follow the stars instead but most off all listen to his inner voice. Scoops greeted the day as the sun rose in the middle of two mountains.

Green trees were in the middle of it. It spread out towards the fountains and flowers below him. Butterflies flew in shades like a rainbow and Scoops realized that this was the place in his mother's story. He finally reached the south.

"Hello! Mom Dad" Scoops shouted

His voice echoed back at him leaving him to wonder if he was wrong then the trees started to ruffle and Scoops kept his eyes on it.

That's when he saw his mom and dad flying towards him along with the rest of the flock Scoops couldn't believe it. He made it to the south. They all gathered around him too glad that he was safe and home with them.

The Mischievous Monkey

Moose swung from one tree to the other whilst screaming from the top of his lungs. He noticed how the other monkeys covered their ears in order not to hear him. That brought a smile to his face. He loved it when everybody was irritated by him he beamed for everyone to see.

They threw him with bananas wanting him to stop. Moose just dived and all their attempts ended up in misses. That always made him laugh and the rest of the monkeys angrier.

"Shut up! They screamed at him as if in a choir

"You guys are so boring! shouted Moose

He gave them one last look dropped to the ground and ran towards the mountaintop. Moose couldn't believe how boring his peers were everything they did was boring. He however needed excitement and knew exactly where to get it. Below him, he saw two other monkeys looking into a honey nest.

Moose's hands were itching he knew he was about to have real fun. He slowly moved down the mountain toward the two other monkeys who were unaware of Moose's approach.

As they leaned in to get a better look inside the nest Moose jumped forward and tied their tails together. Then he picked up a rock and threw it inside the honey nest. Bees came swarming out causing the two monkeys to run in different directions.

They soon realized that they were going nowhere. The birds chirped in alarm as they saw how the two monkeys couldn't get away from the bees as they got stunned. Moose forgot that he had to be silent. He started laughing and that caused the two monkeys to look in his direction.

"Moose how could you! Shouted the monkeys.

But as always all that was visible of Moose was his tail as he ran away not wanting to be caught. Moose was so tired, but his hands were itching to do something mischievous.

"Now that was a lot of fun" beamed Moose.

He wanted more of that he thought to himself. That's when he saw a bird sitting in a tree. He giggled as he slowly moved forward and plucked a feather.

The bird called out in shock as it lost its balance falling from the tree the bird expected the worst. That's when he heard Mooses laugh. And its eyes zoomed in on Moose who made a run for it.

"Moose I'll get you for this," said the bird.

Moose was already gone. Once again only his tail was visible to the bird as he ran not wanting to be caught. There was a mischievous gleam in his eyes as he spotted another victim for his pranks.

A baby Rhino was hiding in the bushes and looked very scared. Moose slowly crawled forward placed his hands and made the sound of a Lion. The little Rhino got such a fright it ran without looking back. Moose was rolling on the ground from laughter.

"What an idiot," said Moose

In his haste, the little Rhino realized that it was Moose and turned around to chase Moose but he was too late. Only a tail sticking out was proof that Moose was at it again.

"I'm gonna tell my parents" Shouted the Rhino

Moose was still laughing when he turned the corner and saw a Tiger drinking water. The sight of a Tiger near the water gave Moose another mischievous idea. He picked up a thick branch and threw it over the tiger's head landing in the water.

The movement and landing of the stick caused the Tiger to jump into the water. But as soon as the Tiger felt the water it tried to jump out.

The Tiger's attempts to get out of the water only made matters worse. It looked bewildered as it moved in haste trying to get to dry land. Moose couldn't believe that a fearless Tiger was looking so silly.

He laughed and that caused the Tiger to stop moving his eyes were now fixated on Moose and it gave an angry roar. Moose looked at the Tiger and pointed at it.

"I'm not scared of you"Shouted Moose.

"I'm gonna get you "replied the Tiger.

That gave Moose a big fright and he started to run again. It wasn't long before only his tail was visible to the Tiger as he moved swiftly from tree to tree.

Moose was now very worried. He had a lot of fun today. But he still had to go home, he wondered who'd be waiting for him.

They all knew his name. That means that he was pretty famous then. Moose smiled at the thought. There was no way they'd be waiting for him Moose assured himself. Though he wasn't so sure of it. He knew he'd had to wait and see.

Moose made his way towards his house. As always he made sure everyone knew he was on his way as he shouted. He didn't notice that the other animals were going into hiding as soon as they heard him approach.

When he finally reached home. He saw that everyone was waiting for him. That made Moose feel proud of himself. It appears as if everyone is ready to give him the respect he deserves for making things interesting in their boring lives.

That thought vanished as soon as he caught a glimpse of his parents next to their leader. He didn't even want to speculate about the unwelcoming glances that were thrown his way.

"Moose " The leader of their tribe gestured for him to come closer.

"Yes sir?" Moose asked in a shaky voice.

He was worried and from the looks of it, he had every reason to be. That is when he looked up and realized that the Rhino, The Bird, the Tiger, the angry monkeys, and the little Elephant were now glaring at him. That is when he realized that he was done for.

"I'm so sorry! I promise not to prank anyone again "stuttered Moose

"Sorry Moose you can't get off that lightly " replied their leader to his confession.

"Yes we can't believe that you got into so much mischief in such a short time." scolded his parents.

Moose hanged his head in shame.

His parents weren't supposed to find out besides it was just harmless fun. He looked at the four standing next to their leader. He had to admit that he might have gone a little bit overboard. He was having too much fun.

"So from now on we will be keeping an eye on you. Their leader informed Moose.

The other monkeys who's been observing everything grabbed Moose on his arms and carried him into a holding room. Their message was clear he was going nowhere until they knew how to deal with him.

Moose knew that he had no choice it seems this time he went too far in his pranks. He was ordered to work for everyone that he pranked or be kicked out of the tribe for his behavior.

As Moose attended to each chore without complaining. He made a promise to himself never to prank anyone again. His mischievous ways were over.

The Firefly Who Couldn't Shine

Pixel the Firefly was sitting on a branch in Pixvalley. She was looking at how the other fireflies flew they were lighting up the sky.

She looked at her light that dimmed slowly and Pixel felt how her chest tighten she couldn't breathe.

She wished with everything in her. That she could be like the other fireflies.Thin and fast, but most of all talkative.

To make matters worse. She didn't feel pretty at all.

Pixel couldn't understand why she felt that way, she just did.

Her wings weren't bright and pretty her legs felt short and fat. Pixel often wondered why she was so different.

"Hey Pixel! Come and fly. Shouted Nanos

"I don't think so, but go on enjoy yourself don't worry about me" replied Pixel

Pixel could see Nanos didn't like being happy while she Pixel sat on the outside looking in. So Pixel quickly dived from the branch and pretended to be happy for her friend's shake. But she felt very unhappy and heavy so she plummeted to the ground.

She watched in horror how her light went out. As Pixel sat in the darkness, she felt very depressed and alone. She wanted to be more like her friend.

Her friend was always the center of attention in short she was beautiful and was their lightning champion.

Pixel sighed she knew it was no one's fault she just couldn't help but compare herself with others and they didn't know it. For that she was grateful. She knew that they would feel terrible if they knew she thought of herself like that.

Pixel flew away from the others, she just wanted to be alone. Her light was dimming now and was very low.

"Why are you going Pixel" Asked the Owl

Pixel nearly hit the tree. That's when she looked up and saw the owl sitting in the tree.

"I'm not feeling like partying " replied Pixel.

"Maybe if you stayed with them, your light will shine brighter. Answered the Owl.

Pixel didn't believe that being around them made her feel even worse about herself.

The Owl just wouldn't understand thought Pixel. He didn't have her problems. She sighed and looked up.

"Even the moon shines brighter than me. Murmured Pixel

The Owl looked up to the sky and saw what Pixel meant. But there was one thing that the firefly was missing, and he decided to tell her.

"That's true, but the moon is all alone, even whilst shining so bright" replied the Owl.

Pixel thought about it and that was true. She wouldn't have liked it if her light shone and she was all alone. That made her feel even more sad. She just can't win thought Pixel.

"Oh well, I'll be on my way. Said Pixel. She flew and looked at the moon that looked so majestic and beautiful, but still all alone.

Pixel was so focused on the moon that she did not see the Jackal running towards the others.

The Jackal knew tonight might be the only chance he got. To grab all of them. He needed their lights to shine for him when he was hunting. He also needs them to be his light in the night. To shine only for him and no one else.

He enviously looked at how brightly they shone. He smiled and reveled in the fact that soon they'd all be his.

He looked down at the bag in his paw and turned when he heard someone approaching.

The jackal looked but couldn't make out anything. He knew that it couldn't be his men. They were told to stay hidden and catch the fireflies who were trying to escape.

He watched the fireflies for a while and jumped out grabbing as many as he could in his paw.

It was chaos as they tried to flee but they couldn't. His men caught the others whilst they were fleeing. The Jackal laughed for him it was a sweet victory.

"Now you're all mine" he grimaced

It didn't bother the Jackal that he had just turned everything into darkness. The moon and stars were the only light.

Pixel was sitting on a leaf and realized that she was so lost in thought that she didn't even hear the happy chatter of the other fireflies.

She frowned it was way too early for the festivity to stop. In all the years it was never so quiet.

Pixel couldn't understand it but she was worried and needed to find out why she was feeling that way. As Pixel flew back she saw that the garden was empty and dark. She knew something must have happened. Only she didn't know what. Pixel heard the branches move and shrieked.

"Huh! Who's there, come out whomever you are. demanded Pixel.

What she saw next made her sigh with relief. It was zebras stumbling over each other.

"What happened why is it so dark here?," asked one Zebra

"Isn't there supposed to be a festival here" Continued the other.

"I'm still trying to figure out why everyone is gone all of a sudden," said Pixel

Pixel wanted to explain further. But there was another ruffling sound. She knew she wouldn't have the patience if she was asked another question.

"Pssst up here! Whispered the owl.

It was a relief for Pixel to see a familiar face. Though she wondered if she made him worry too much. Why else would he come to check up on her?

"Wise one, you don't have to worry about me, as you can see I'm quite fine " Pixel Assured him.

She didn't want the Zebras to know how she felt earlier. But that answer seems to have a confusing effect on the Owl.

"No!No! Dear I'm not here about that, said the Owl.

"Oh, I guess whatever it is must be important for you to come all this way " replied Pixel

The Owl wondered if he should tell the firefly about what happened. She wasn't doing so well.

What can she do she is just one firefly. But then he decided if he helped her they could do a lot to save the rest of the fireflies.

"Yes it is, I saw that lazy Jackal and his pack catching the fireflies and throwing them into bags" replied the Owl

Pixel was too shocked to respond what could he want with them? What he did was horrible and Pixel could feel how her chest was tightening she fought it off now was not the time for her to feel sorry for herself.

Her family and friends needed her. She just wondered how she was going to handle them all on her own and free the others.

"Don't worry we'll help you free them" said the Owl

"Sure thing! We'll get the others to come and help," said Zebra

As they moved deeper into the forest. The Owl and Zebras woke everyone that they could to help with their rescue mission. Pixel could not help it she was very glad that she had met the Owl earlier.

She was filled with so much joy, she had a lot of help and she was not alone. She also noticed that it wasn't so dark after all a bright light was lighting their path.

When she looked to see where it came from she realized that the light came from her.

"I'm glowing" she yelled.

She turned to find the owl. He was already looking at her with a proud smile. Pixel had no words after all this time she was just like all the other fireflies.

"All you needed was to believe in yourself," said the Owl knowingly.

As she flew and lightened the path for the others. Pixel decided not to doubt herself again or think less of herself, she has been unhappy for no reason.

As they neared the Jackal's lair they could hear the Jackal boasting to his followers amidst the bright lights that shone on them from the fireflies. Their wings were tied up so they couldn't fly away. That made Pixel very angry.

"Jackal let my people go" demanded Pixel.

Jackal turned and looked at Pixel, he was ready to grab her too. Though his paw froze in mid-air when he noticed that she wasn't alone.

Zebra and all the others surrounded the Jackal and his team. Then they started to move in.

They weren't about to let a scoundrel like the Jackal escape. They wanted to teach him a lesson. They all suffered in the darkness because of his actions.

The Jackal couldn't believe that so many showed up to help the fireflies and he stepped backward.

Not wanting them to come closer. He panicked when he saw that he was about to be cornered.

He didn't bargain on his plan going wrong and never dreamed that he would be the one on the losing end.

Maybe his plan was not as tight as he had thought. While he moved back he kept his eyes on the others looking for an escape route.

There's one thing that he was sure of not one of them would be able to catch him thought the Jackal slyly. He quickly turned and made a run for it, before anyone could grab him.

"Untie them! He ordered the other Jackals as he fled.

Whom immediately did as they were told.

Once the fireflies were untied they were chased away with their tails between their legs. They didn't even bother to look back too afraid that the rest might be following them.

Don't miss out!

Visit the website below and you can sign up to receive emails whenever Mary-Ann Storm publishes a new book. There's no charge and no obligation.

https://books2read.com/r/B-A-SKLF-FWVKC

BOOKS2READ

Connecting independent readers to independent writers.

Also by Mary-Ann Storm

Dinno's Adventure And Other Tales
Solace
I'm A Woman

About the Author

Mary-Ann Storm is a Journalist and writer from South Africa. She was born in Ceres but grew up in the Overberg Region in the Western Cape.

www.ingramcontent.com/pod-product-compliance
Lightning Source LLC
Chambersburg PA
CBHW072043150726

47996CB00014B/1360